Dancing
For Ever

Miss Coralie turned to me and her eyes and voice were so full of strictness it was scary. "Rose, I shouldn't need to have to say this to you, and I hope I don't need to have to say it again. Do not let yourself get distracted. You're doing grade four this term. You won't pass unless you put one hundred per cent of yourself into your work."

Ballerina Dreams

Collect all the books in the series:

Poppy's Secret Wish

Jasmine's Lucky Star

Rose's Big Decision

Dancing with the Stars

Dancing Princess

Coming Soon

The Christmas Nutcracker

Ballerina Dreams

Dancing For Ever

Ann Bryant

USBORNE

For my stepdaughter, Becky, with love.

The publisher would like to thank Sara Matthews of the
Central School of Ballet for her assistance.

First published in the UK in 2005 by Usborne Publishing Ltd,
Usborne House, 83-85 Saffron Hill, London EC1N 8RT, England.
www.usborne.com

Cover photograph by Ray Moller.
Illustrations by Tim Benton.
The name Usborne and the devices ♀ ⊕ are Trade Marks
of Usborne Publishing Ltd. All rights reserved.

A CPI catalogue record for this title is available
from the British Library.

JF AMJJASOND/05
ISBN 0 7460 6435 7

Printed in Great Britain.

1 The Boy

Mum grabbed the car keys and called out to Jack, my eldest brother, that we were going, then turned to me. "Ready, Rose?"

I was practising my *chassé coupé* exercise in the kitchen, but I stopped straight away, grabbed my ballet bag and followed her out of the house. I love this time, every Tuesday after school, when I know I'm just about to have the best hour of my whole week. I go to the Coralie Charlton School of Ballet. Miss Coralie is the teacher and she's very strict, but also totally brilliant. In fact, she used to be in the Royal

Ballet Company before she set up her own ballet school. She's entered me for the grade four exam at the end of this term, and I can't wait because if I pass I'll be back in the same class as my two best friends, Jasmine and Poppy. They did their grade four last year, but I'm a bit behind because I've not been doing ballet for as long as them. I'm so nervous about the exam. I've just *got* to pass it. I've been practising like mad and working my very hardest in every single ballet class.

As I got in the car, I remembered something that Miss Coralie had said in the last lesson.

"Mum," I blurted out, "there's going to be a boy in the class today."

"That's unusual," she replied.

She was certainly right about that. Jasmine and Poppy had told me that there used to be quite a few boys in grade one, but I didn't go to ballet then. In fact, I only joined last year when I was in Year Five, and went straight into grade four. I was such a tomboy and I absolutely hated the thought of ballet, but my granny had bought me a term's lessons for my birthday and Mum had booked me in at Miss Coralie's, so I didn't have much choice in the matter.

Looking back now, I can't believe Miss Coralie even let me join grade four. I was hopeless and I must have looked ridiculous with my leotard in wrinkles because it was too big for me, and my hair in tangles because I hadn't realized how neat you have to look. Mum says Miss Coralie must have been really clever to have seen my potential just from the audition I did. I'm *so* glad that my granny got me those lessons in the first place. I'm totally serious about ballet now. My dream is to be a soloist in a ballet company like the Royal Ballet, and for Poppy and Jasmine to be soloists too. Then we could still be the "triplegang", as I call it, just like we are now.

✳

In the changing room everyone was talking about the new boy.

"Where's he going to change? Better not be in here!" giggled a girl called Becky.

"It'll be so weird having a boy in class, won't it?" said Becky's friend, Emily, in a really silly voice.

Personally, I didn't see why it should be any different from having a new girl in class. But that's probably because I mainly used to hang out with boys at school last year and I've got three older brothers so I'm used to boys.

"I wonder if he'll have special exercises to do," said Becky.

Nobody really knew the answer to that and anyway it was time for us to line up in the corridor. I stood in front of the mirror to check that I looked completely neat and tidy without even a millimetre of pants showing, or a single bump in my hair, then went out of the changing room with the others. And that was when I got a shock, because coming out of the little room next to Miss Coralie's office was a boy called Kieran Steel, who started in 6L at school at the beginning of this term. And that's my class! He was wearing black shorts, a black T-shirt and black ballet shoes.

"Ooh!" said Emily, in her silly voice, which made everyone giggle.

I wanted to make up for her being rude, so I said, "Hi! Are you the new boy?"

It was a pretty stupid thing to say because of course he was the new boy. I could feel lots of eyes darting from me to Kieran, and Kieran himself looked a bit embarrassed. He seemed to be checking all the faces in the line, then he looked back at me.

"You can stand in front of me, if you want," I said, shuffling back a bit to let him in. I was remembering my own first few lessons. "It's horrible when you're new and you don't know anyone, isn't it?"

He gave me a half smile and looked as though he was about to reply, but then Miss Coralie called out, "Come in, class," and we were all instantly silent as we ran in very lightly and found a place at the *barre.*

"This is Kieran, everyone," said Miss Coralie. "He's joining us from another ballet school and it might take him a little while to get used to the syllabus we do here. Prepare the arm for *pliés...* And..."

I couldn't help my eyes flicking over to the mirror all the time, so I could watch Kieran. He was quite good at the actual steps. He just didn't know how to fit them to the music. I'd never seen a boy of my age doing ballet before, apart from in the film, *Billy Elliot,* and I kept picturing Kieran in the classroom at school, surrounded by his mates, and on the football pitch where everyone wants him on their team because he's such a good player. It was surprising that boys like Archie Cook and Tom

Priest didn't mind having a friend who went to ballet. You'd have thought they'd leave him out of their games and be really mean to him. It was bad enough when *I* first started ballet – they teased me like mad. And I'm a *girl*.

"And the other side," said Miss Coralie, so we all turned to face the other way. Now I could easily watch Kieran without him realizing because he was in front of me, His hair was incredibly short. I think it's called a *number one* when it's nearly all shaved off like that. Mum only lets my brothers have *number threes* because she thinks *number ones* make you look too hard.

For the centre work, Kieran was put in between me and Emily in the second row. He did some brilliant *jetés* and I whispered to him, "That was good!" We're not actually allowed to say a single word in class because Miss Coralie is so strict, but she was telling Mrs. Marsden, the pianist, something at that moment.

"Thanks!" Kieran answered with a grin. Then he hissed into the back of my head, "Boys can jump higher than girls."

I so wanted to put him right on that one, but I kept completely quiet and still because Miss Coralie was turning back round.

"Right, let's have the *chassé coupé* exercise," she said briskly. "It's a different exercise for boys, Kieran, so just stand to the side."

This was the exercise that I'd been practising and I was dying to see if I could get all the way through it without Miss Coralie correcting me. We have to do it round the room and I was chosen to go first. I stood in third position with my arms in *fifth en bas* and waited for the music. If you've never done ballet, it's impossible to explain how difficult it is to make steps like this look as though you're really dancing on a stage, but at the same time make sure you've got the technique absolutely right.

"Lovely, Rose!" said Miss Coralie.

Miss Coralie only ever says that if she's really impressed, so I was over the moon, and couldn't wait to tell Poppy and Jasmine. I glanced across at Kieran and he did a few little silent claps as though he was saying *Well done!* Then when we were about to have another go, I caught sight of him watching me. *So you think boys can jump higher than girls, do you Kieran?* I thought. *Well, watch this!* I sprung up as high as I could, even though it stopped me having such a good position when I landed.

"Not bad!" said Kieran out of the side of his mouth as we swapped places. I couldn't help giggling because he looked so funny, like a ventriloquist without a dummy.

"Good, Kieran," said Miss Coralie, when he'd finished his special boys' step and was standing with a straight back and knees locked tight. "Just make sure your weight is equally balanced when you land each time."

Kieran waited till her back was turned, then

licked his finger and drew a number 1 in the air as though he was keeping score of how many compliments we both got from Miss Coralie. Then he suddenly dropped into a *plié* with bent legs, shifted his balance and lifted one leg up, so he looked like a mad frog, cross-eyed, with his mouth wide open. He was showing exactly how you *shouldn't* land and I couldn't help letting out a giggle. But a second later Miss Coralie turned back to face us, and quick as a flash Kieran stood up straight.

It was great having Kieran in class. I couldn't wait to tell Poppy and Jasmine about how funny he was, and how good he was at ballet too. And the next day at school Poppy would be able to meet him properly. She's in the other Year Six class. I was sure she'd really like him.

Later in the ballet class Kieran had to demonstrate a sequence of jumps in first and second position. It was incredible how high he managed to jump without leaning forwards when he landed, and I could see lots of girls looking very impressed. It was good fun doing it a row at a time because I had a little competition with myself to see if I could jump as high as him.

The more the class went on, the more I wished my brothers could see Kieran dancing. They're always teasing me about how ballet is for girls, and boys are too tough for such a girlie thing, but I'd like to see them try to do half the things Kieran could do. They'd be pathetic at it.

I suddenly realized I'd been in my own little world, not concentrating at all, so I quickly pulled myself up straight. I must have overdone it, though.

"Relax your shoulders, Rose," said Miss Coralie, "and soften your arms. You look like a sergeant major!"

Then she turned to have a word with Mrs. Marsden, and fast as anything Kieran gave me a salute, clicking his heels together. I tried so hard to stifle my giggle but it didn't work and Miss Coralie swung round and frowned. Kieran, of course, was wearing a completely straight face like everyone else in the class. But I was standing there grinning like an idiot.

All the same, it was Kieran she spoke to. "You've got a lot of catching up to do, and you *don't* have time for messing around. Is that clear?"

Kieran nodded but then I got a shock because Miss Coralie turned to me and her eyes and voice were so full of strictness it was scary. "Rose, I shouldn't need to have to say this to you, and I hope I don't need to have to say it again. Do *not* let yourself get distracted. You're doing grade four this term. You won't pass unless you put one hundred per cent of yourself into your work."

I nodded and felt my face turning pale because her eyes were still on me and I couldn't look away.

2 The Big Know-all Brothers

At the end of the class everybody filed out past the line of grade five girls who were about to go in for their own class. I was two behind Kieran and I saw Poppy stare as she realized who it was, but Jazz was raising her eyebrows at me as if to say, *Who's the boy?* Then as they went into their class, Kieran headed for the little room next to Miss Coralie's office.

"Got my own personal changing room as I'm such a star," he said, grinning all over his face.

I came out of the line too then.

"Brilliant balancing frog, by the way, Kieran!"

I was expecting him to grin at me, but instead his face clouded over. "I'm not going to muck about any more. I'm here to learn ballet."

It was amazing the way Kieran could be joking one minute and deadly serious the next.

"And by the way, people don't know I do ballet," he suddenly blurted out.

"What people?"

He looked at the floor. "The boys at school... You know..."

"The boys you hang around with?"

"Yeah." He looked me straight in the eyes. "And I want to keep it that way. So don't tell anyone, okay?"

"Okay. I won't say anything."

"Not even your friend...what's her name?"

"Poppy wouldn't tell anyone. I can promise you that. It makes me mad, though, that you have to hide your ballet when you're so good at it. I mean, none of those boys at school could do anything like you can. I used to hang out with most of them last year before I started doing ballet, but Poppy and Jazz are my best friends now. They completely understand about ballet. You can talk to me and Poppy at break times if you like."

"You're joking! No way! When we're at school, you just keep away from me, like you don't know me from out of school."

Then he turned and went into his changing room and I was left there feeling strange and a bit sad.

That evening I phoned Jasmine. We nearly always phone each other on Tuesday evenings because she goes to a different school from me and Poppy, and I only get to see her properly at weekends. She's got the strictest father known to man, you see, and he doesn't let her have friends round during the week.

"The new boy, Kieran, is such good fun, Jazz. You should have seen his balancing frog act!"

"Did he do it during class? Didn't Miss Coralie go mad?"

"No, it's okay, she didn't see. We made really sure we only mucked about behind her back."

Jasmine gasped. "You can't muck about in class, Rose! You've got the exam coming up."

"I know... We weren't exactly mucking about..."

"But you will be careful, won't you? You'll get told off..."

It was a good job Jasmine couldn't see my guilty face. I thought I ought to say something to show the serious side of Kieran, and right on cue a brilliant idea popped into my head.

"He used to do a different syllabus at his old class and I was thinking, wouldn't it be good if he came round on Saturday with you and Poppy, so we can help him learn the steps?"

There was a pause. I guessed Jasmine wasn't too sure about having a boy round, when it had always just been us three.

"You and Poppy are such good teachers, Jazz. And just think how impressed Miss Coralie would be if Kieran came back next week knowing everything perfectly!"

Jasmine laughed then and said that she didn't think he'd get that far in just one week. But now, at least she didn't seem to mind about him coming round. So as soon as I'd put the phone down, I told Mum my plan and she said it would be fine for him to come on Saturday.

"I don't want the boys teasing him or anything, though, Mum. I just know they'll find it totally weird that Kieran does ballet."

"Well, you're in luck because Rory and Adam have both got away matches and Jack'll be in his room studying for his exams."

Phew! That was a big relief. So then I started telling Mum all about Kieran.

"You should see him in class, Mum..."

But I didn't get any further because Adam

and Rory had come into the kitchen and I hadn't even realized.

A big smirk was forming on Adam's face. "Don't tell me there's a boy at Miss Coronary's?"

I hate it when they call Miss Coralie that and it made me so mad because my brothers are never normally interested in anything I talk about.

"What's his name?" Rory asked, grinning all over his stupid face.

"Kieran," said Mum. Then she saw me looking fed up and spoke to the boys a bit snappily. "What do you two want, anyway? You're not still hungry, I hope."

But neither of them answered because Rory was creased up watching Adam twirling round in a really stupid way with his arms above his head. "Hello," he said in a high-pitched voice, "my name's Kieran and I do ballet!"

I felt like hitting Adam really hard, but I made myself keep calm because I know from bitter experience that they only get worse if I show that I'm mad.

"Don't be so silly, Adam," Mum said, but you could tell she wasn't really paying attention to us lot any more. Then she mumbled something about getting the washing in and went out of the back door.

The moment she'd gone, Rory yanked the freezer door open to help himself to ice cream, and Adam began jumping from foot to foot, pointing the other foot in front, looking completely clumsy and terrible. I didn't say a word, just went to walk out, but I only got as far as the doorway because I bumped into my oldest brother, Jack.

"Very serious face, Ro. What's up?" Jack asked. But then he must have caught sight of Adam. "What's going on?"

"Adam's being totally moronic because..." I stopped mid-sentence. What if Jack started teasing me about Kieran too?

"Because there's a new boy in Ro's ballet class!" said Rory.

Jack broke into a grin and sat down at the table. I couldn't believe it. Even *he* found it funny. I was furious.

"If you lot saw him dance, you wouldn't make jokes about him, you know. He's really good."

Out of the corner of my eye I could see Adam doing those stupid jumps again, only this time he had stiff arms above his head. Jack was trying to hide his smirk and I wanted to kill all three of them then.

My voice came out really stressily. "I bet he's stronger than any of you lot, and he's definitely more supple, *and* he's got ten times more energy, so I don't know what's so funny!"

"Look, Ro," said Rory, as though he was having to explain something to a little kid who wasn't getting it, "I don't know why you go on about ballet dancers. They don't have to get through ninety minutes or more of running and dodging round a football pitch, you know, and I'm telling you, that's far tougher than doing a few little jumps."

Sometimes it makes me mad being the only girl in a family of big know-all brothers, and this was one of those times. They had no idea how special Kieran must be, to have joined a class of girls at his age, and to be really talented at something that most boys don't even dare to do in case anyone accuses them of being girlie. And I was also annoyed because they just didn't have a clue about how much strength and stamina male ballet dancers need to have. I just wished I could prove it somehow.

3 Friends

The moment the bell went for morning break at school the next day, I shot out to the playground to find Poppy.

"I've got something important to tell you about Kieran," I said in a whispered gabble as I led her away from any big ears. "You see, he absolutely doesn't want any of the boys to find out he does ballet, so don't breathe a word, okay?"

Poppy's eyes grew big. "Poor him," she said quietly, looking over to where Kieran was in the middle of a game of football with most of the

Year Six boys. "But tell me what he's like. Is he good at ballet? Where did he go to classes before?"

"He's really good fun and he's great at ballet. He can jump so high you'd think he'd got magic powers or something. But I haven't the faintest idea where he used to go to classes. I've got loads of things I want to ask him, but it's impossible when I'm not even allowed to talk to him."

Poppy went a bit pink under her freckles. "I'm glad I'm not a boy," she said. "I'd hate to have to keep ballet a secret."

Then I remembered my plan. "I'm going to ask him over on Saturday so he can meet you and Jazz. We could help him with the grade four steps, couldn't we? It'd be great, wouldn't it?"

Poppy's eyes were full of doubt and worry. "Are you sure, Rose? Do you think he'd really want to do ballet with three girls?"

"Yes I do, actually. He's just as serious as

we are." But then I suddenly had a picture of Kieran dancing away with us three, and I wondered whether Poppy might be right after all. I mean, it was one thing practising on your own, but it was a bit different practising with three girls. I still wanted him to come though because he was my new buddy in class. It was all right for Jasmine and Poppy, they'd got each other in grade five.

"Well, we don't have to do ballet *all* the time, do we?" I said carefully.

Now she looked really alarmed. "But we *always* do ballet all the time. Jasmine would definitely want to."

"Well, we could do it *most* of the time. But just not absolutely *all* of it. It'll be fine, you'll see."

Poppy still didn't look too sure.

"I'm sure you and Jazz will really like him," I said, grabbing her hands and dancing her round. "He really made me giggle when he pretended to be a mad frog!"

The moment the words were out of my mouth I wished I could shovel them back in again because Poppy was looking as horrified as Jazz had sounded on the phone.

"You won't let him distract you in class, will you, Rose? You've got grade four soon, remember."

Of course I remembered. And it was really starting to bug me the way Jazz and Poppy were acting like my parents when they were supposed to be my best friends. I couldn't help snapping a bit.

"He doesn't distract me, okay? Anyway, I'm going to see if he's free next weekend."

I started striding over towards the boys' football game, but luckily Poppy yanked me back and started hissing in my ear.

"What are you doing, Rose? You're not supposed to know him all that well, remember?"

I clapped my hand over my mouth. "Oh no! I forgot!"

Poppy smiled at me then. A bit of a grown-up smile, but at least it was a smile, so I grinned back. She needn't have worried about me. I would never let Kieran or *anybody* get in the way of my ballet progress, and right now grade four is the most important thing in my life.

In the end Kieran *didn't* come on Saturday because I never got the chance to ask him at school. Poppy and Jazz and I had a brilliant time on our own, though. Jack said I could look through his CDs and we chose a piece called *Albatross.* There weren't any words but it was the most beautiful music, and our new dance turned out to be one of the best we'd ever choreographed. Well, actually Jazz did most of the choreography as usual, because she's so good at it.

"What shall we call it?" asked Poppy with shiny eyes, when we knew the sequence really well.

"What about something simple like *Trio?*" Jazz said.

I agreed that that was a great title, and we danced it through again and again.

"If Kieran comes over next weekend, he can watch us dance this," I said.

I wasn't expecting Poppy and Jazz to jump for joy exactly, but I did kind of hope they'd be a *little* bit excited.

"We ought to meet at my house next weekend," said Poppy, "because Mum and Stevie will be out and Dad'll probably be gardening all the time."

That was great news. "Yay! That means Kieran won't have to put up with my pesty pain brothers."

"So...he'd be coming to *my* house?" Poppy was going pink again. She always does if she's a bit embarrassed or even surprised or worried.

"Are you sure he'll...fit in with us lot?" asked Jazz, biting her lip.

Poppy screwed up her face as though she was picturing him. "I can't imagine him actually sitting down and watching us dance. He's always racing round the playground when I see him."

I didn't get what they were so worried about. "He really wants to learn the new syllabus, you know." I put on a bit of a hurt face on purpose.

"It'll probably be all right," said Jazz hesitantly as Poppy put her arm round me.

"Yes, I absolutely *know* it will," I said excitedly, as though we'd definitely agreed that he was coming. "Now, let's find some really good music that we can practise jumps to. I'm dying to see if I can..." But I stopped myself finishing that sentence because it was stupid of me to think about having jumping competitions with Kieran. I definitely wasn't going to let him distract me any more.

Definitely.

4 Bird of Prey

On Tuesday, as ballet drew nearer I got more and more excited at the thought of being in class with Kieran. And by the time we were ready to line up in the corridor, my whole body was buzzing.

I concentrated hard all through the *barre* work and got a "nice" from Miss Coralie. Kieran was at the other end of the *barre*, so I couldn't look at him but I hoped he noticed that *I'd* got the first compliment from Miss Coralie.

During the *port de bras*, I managed to get a "very nice, Rose". I really wanted to lick my finger and pretend to write the number 1 in the air like Kieran had done, but he wasn't watching so there was no point. I kept my eye on him though, and the moment he looked across in my direction I did it. Unfortunately, Miss Coralie saw me.

"Rose?"

She'd only said my name but her eyes seemed to be flashing a warning, so I quickly stood up straight ready for the next exercise.

Then it was time for the jumps – my favourite part of the lesson. Miss Coralie talked us through a sequence of *jetés* and *assemblés,* and when we did it a row at a time Kieran did it absolutely brilliantly and got a "Lovely!" from Miss Coralie. I kept on waiting for him to look at me but he never did and I couldn't help feeling a bit disappointed. This lesson wasn't half as good as the last one.

At the end of the lesson we don't normally make a proper line. It just kind of forms itself.

And no one usually talks, partly because we're all so tired, but mainly because Miss Coralie likes us to be nice and calm on our way to the changing room. Today I was almost at the back of the line, but Kieran was up near the front. I was desperate to get his attention before he went into his changing room so I could invite him to Poppy's house on Saturday, but even though I kept bobbing my head from side to side hoping he'd turn round and see me, he never did, and he'd disappeared into his changing room before I could catch up with him. I decided the next best thing would be to get changed double quick and wait for him at the bottom of the stairs. So the moment I'd snapped the velcro straps on my trainers I rushed off down the echoey staircase.

I love these stairs, especially when there's no one else on them. They spiral round for ever with corners instead of bends, and today I pretended I was a bird swooping down on my prey, my arms stretched like wings. It was wicked. But I stopped on the fifth spiral because I'd suddenly realized something terrible. I'd been so wrapped up trying to attract Kieran's attention at the end of class that I hadn't even noticed Poppy and Jasmine in the line. How stupid of me! We *always* exchange looks when they're lined up ready to go into their class. Every single week. I slumped my shoulders forwards and dropped my head back with my mouth open, which is my cross-with-myself position. And it was right then that I realized someone was higher up the staircase. I looked up properly to see Kieran three spirals above me.

"Trying to catch flies, Rose? I just saw your bird act, by the way!"

He was grinning all over his face and I quickly shut my mouth and tried to look cool. I thought he'd say something else to tease me, but instead he stretched his own arms out and did that same tumble running thing that I'd been doing. By the time he got down to me he was laughing. I was glad he was back to his old self.

"Good fun, isn't it?" I said.

He didn't answer, just grinned, and we walked the last spiral together.

"I was wondering if you wanted to come round to Poppy's on Saturday," I said. "She's the one I hang around with at school. And Jazz is coming too. They're both in grade five... They're really nice."

Kieran looked a bit doubtful.

"They could help you learn the syllabus. They're brilliant teachers. They helped me like mad when I didn't know it."

"Poppy hasn't got any brothers or sisters at school, has she? I'm not coming if there's any chance of it getting back to the Year Six boys."

"She's got a little brother but he's going to be out all day."

There was a long pause while Kieran frowned and stared into thin air. Then finally he said, "Okay. I'll ask Mum."

"Brill!"

And it *would* be. I couldn't wait.

5 Broken Spells

"Are you sure he knows where I live?" squeaked Poppy, for the fifth time.

We were in the middle of her living room with all the furniture pushed back against the walls, and getting completely hyper because Kieran would be arriving at any moment. It was great that Poppy and Jazz were just as excited as me.

"I'm a bit nervous," Jazz admitted.

"Me too," Poppy said. "What if he doesn't get on with us at all?"

"He will!" I told them, sticking out my two thumbs.

And each of them straight away touched my thumbs with theirs, and then touched their other thumbs together so we were all connected in a circle. This is our special good luck signal that we call a thumb-thumb.

Poppy broke away first and sounded a bit anxious again. "You *are* sure he'll want to do ballet, aren't you, Rose?"

I didn't have to answer her because the front doorbell rang just then, and we all jumped about half a mile in the air.

"He's here!" said Jazz in a trembly voice.

She and Poppy stood there clutching each other so I rushed to open the door.

"Oh good, we've found the right house," were Kieran's first words. Then he turned round and gave his mum a thumbs-up. She smiled and waved from the car so I waved back because Kieran had walked straight past me into the hall. I noticed he was wearing jogging bottoms, a T-shirt and trainers, but he'd got a small rucksack with him.

"Hi," Poppy and Jazz said shyly when we were all in the living room.

Kieran grinned at them and dropped his bag. "So this is what you do then? Push all the furniture back and practise ballet?"

"We're usually in Poppy's bedroom, but as there's no one around, we thought we'd come in here," Jazz explained.

"Cool," said Kieran.

"We made up a really good dance last weekend," Poppy blurted out. "We've called it *Trio*. Do you want to see it?"

I was really pleased that so far Poppy and Jazz seemed to like Kieran.

"Yeah, okay," he said. "What's the music?"

"It's called *Albatross*," I told him.

He grinned at me. "Bet I know why you chose that one, Rose! You like pretending to be a bird, don't you?"

I giggled, remembering how I'd run down the

stairs at ballet with my arms stretched out.

"So do *you!*"

"Yeah, but I don't try to catch flies!" Kieran said. Then he picked up something from Poppy's sideboard. "What's this?"

"It's just one of those puzzles where you have to work out how to separate the bits of metal," said Poppy quickly. I could tell she was dying to get on with the dance because she was standing in her starting position.

"Shall I put the music on?" asked Jazz.

But Kieran was totally into the puzzle. "Have you done it?" he asked, without looking up.

"Yes, but I'd never be able to remember how," said Poppy.

I knew *I'd* be able to remember because I'd done it quite a few times. "Do you want me to show you, Kieran?" I asked.

"No, I want to do it myself."

I couldn't resist turning it into a game. "Right,

I'll time you. If you can't do it in less than a minute, you're not as good as me!"

"Game on!" said Kieran.

A little surge of excitement raced through me. I'd heard that expression loads of times at home. It was Jack who'd first said it, when he'd been racing caterpillars with Rory, and his caterpillar had suddenly gone into the lead. Since then we'd all started saying "Game on!" whenever we were trying to outdo each other. The rule in our house is that if someone says it, the other person has to say, "Lay your bets!" and then the two people shake hands, even if there's no actual bet. So, without thinking, I stuck out my hand to Kieran.

"Lay your bets."

"Twenty pence says I can do it under a minute."

We shook on it.

"Get ready!" I instructed him, looking at my watch. "And...go!"

That was when I realized that Jazz and Poppy were looking rather fed up.

"After this we'll do the dance," I quickly said, with a big smile to cheer them up.

Twenty-eight seconds later, Kieran was punching the air with his fist as though he'd just broken a world record.

"I haven't got any money," I told him a bit sulkily. Then to change the subject I said, "Hey, why don't you show Jazz and Poppy your balancing frog act!"

"It's not all that funny…"

"Look, shall we get on with the grade four work now?" That was Jasmine and she sounded a bit annoyed.

"I thought you were going to show me your bird dance," said Kieran, grinning at me.

"It's not a bird dance," said Poppy, going a bit pink. "The music's called *Albatross*, that's all."

So Kieran sat on the settee, Poppy put on the CD and we all took up our positions. The dance is quite a serious one. You see, when we choreograph things, we don't just put a whole string of steps together, we try to make the dance have a meaning, and *Trio* is supposed to be about making and breaking friendships. I have to start in a low shape with my head down. But the moment I got into position I felt a giggle springing about inside my stomach because of the thought of Kieran's balancing frog, and no matter how hard I tried to bury it, I couldn't. I managed to dance for about fifteen seconds before I burst into hysterical laughter.

Poppy and Jazz shot very impatient looks at me and Jazz's lips were really tight.

"S...sorry," I spluttered. "I was th...thinking about the frog."

Kieran sighed. "Come on, Rose. Get a grip!"

So Poppy put the CD back on, and I tried like mad to concentrate, but I didn't even last fifteen seconds this time.

"It's no good, I can't stop thinking about it

now," I said, flopping down on the settee next to Kieran. "Sorry, everyone."

Poppy and Jazz looked totally fed up with me by then.

"We'll come back to it later," said Jazz in quite a cross voice.

"Do you want to show me some grade four stuff?" said Kieran, reaching into his bag and pulling out his ballet shoes.

Jazz and Poppy looked much happier then, and after no time at all I could tell that they were really impressed with Kieran. We all held on to the backs of the chairs and the settee for the *barre* and I did my own practice while Jazz and Poppy helped Kieran with the steps. I loved being in my own little world, trying to do better and better, feeling strong and calm, both at once. But then Kieran broke in on my concentration by tickling the back of my leg with the toe of his ballet shoe in the middle of one of his exercises.

"Get off, Kieran!" I said, turning round and scowling.

But a moment later I was laughing because he immediately gave me his sergeant major salute, clicking his heels together and standing really straight.

I saw Jazz and Poppy sighing a bit, but they weren't cross like they had been before. Their sighs were only because we'd all been deep in our ballet worlds, and then the spell had somehow been broken.

Later, when Kieran had gone Poppy said, "He's nice, isn't he?"

"And he's very good at ballet," Jazz added.

But then they ruined it.

"You've got to be careful you don't let him distract you though, Rose," Poppy said, hesitantly.

"You don't want Miss Coralie to pull you out of the exam or anything." That was Jazz. In a very soft voice.

"She can't. She's already entered me," I replied a bit huffily.

But a shiver ran over my body. And I was cross because it felt as if another spell had been broken.

6 Doggy's Assault Course

I was so excited when Kieran phoned the next day to see if I could go over to his place. Mum drove me there and Kieran's mum invited her to stay for a cup of tea.

"I'm Maria," she said in her soft voice. Then Kieran appeared. He was wearing jeans and the same T-shirt again, and his feet were bare.

"Let's go up to my room."

As we went upstairs, I realized that I didn't actually know anything about Kieran except that he loved ballet, was great at games, quite good at school work, and liked joking around.

"Have you got any brothers or sisters?" I asked him.

He shook his head. "Have you?"

So then we went through loads of details about our lives and I found out that he used to live in Ireland but his mum had separated from his dad and they'd decided to come to England.

"Do you want to make ballet your career?" I said.

"Uh-huh. Do you?"

"Yes, definitely. I love it more than anything in the whole world."

Kieran looked as though he'd suddenly made a decision. "I've got something to show you. Come on."

"Oh right..." I followed him as he whizzed downstairs.

When we got to the bottom, Mum and Maria were just coming out of the kitchen.

"I'm off now, love," Mum said. "I'll be back at six-thirty."

"Okay." Then I turned to Kieran. "Where are we going?"

"You'll see."

We went through the kitchen and out of the back door to a shed in the garden. Kieran opened the door and grinned. "Look." He pointed to a thick metal pull-up bar above his head. "This is good for strengthening upper body muscles, see."

He jumped up and grabbed the bar with his hands, then pulled himself up and lowered himself down loads of times, his feet never touching the floor.

I was desperate for him to see that I was strong too, because of all my gym. "Can I have a go?"

"Yeah." He dropped to the ground and watched me.

I managed five, but my arms weren't as strong as they used to be now I was doing so much less gym. I didn't think Poppy or Jasmine would be able to do more than one because they've never done any arm strengthening work at all.

"What's the most you can do, Kieran?"

"Twenty."

He wasn't showing off, he was just telling me. Then I spotted a ball thing hanging from a metal frame that had been screwed into the wall. "What's that?"

"It's a speed ball. Boxers use them to train."

"Oh, wow! Show me!"

He put on a pair of boxing gloves and began punching quickly.

"Hey, that's brilliant! Can I have a go?"

"You're the first girl who's ever wanted a go on my stuff," he said, looking quite pleased, I thought.

I put on the gloves and started stabbing away like Kieran had done, but it didn't work at all for me. I kept punching the air instead of the ball.

"You have to get into a rhythm," Kieran explained. He showed me how to do it slowly, then gradually build up to a faster speed.

I tried again, but I still wasn't much good so I went back to the pull-up bar.

"You're not bad...for a girl," said Kieran, when I dropped down to the floor after I'd managed eight quick pull-ups. Then he suddenly turned serious. "Do you want to see something that no one else has seen, apart from Mum?"

I nodded, wondering what on earth it was going to be. In a flash he whipped an old blanket out of the way and there was a ballet *barre*. I couldn't believe my eyes.

"You come out here to practise ballet?"

"Yeah. There's not enough room in the house for a *barre*. And anyway, I wouldn't want anyone to see it." A second later, he'd thrown the blanket back over the *barre* and was looking at me with excited eyes. "Do you want to see Doggy's assault course?"

My head was spinning. "What? Who's Doggy?"

"It's a dog that we kind of adopted," he explained, going out of the shed and back into the garden. "When we lived in Ireland, he just turned up out of nowhere one day and we took him to the police and everything, but no one ever claimed him, so we kept him. We'd been calling him Doggy for so long by then, he thought it was his name. He's still getting used to living over here."

"Where is he?" I asked, looking round the garden. Then I spotted a few things lying around that I hadn't noticed before. "And what's that broom doing there and that thick plastic sheet?"

Kieran whistled very softly through his teeth and a scruffy-looking, dark grey mongrel came out from behind the shed at the bottom of the garden.

"Here, Doggy! Fun time!" In a flash, the dog was sitting beside Kieran looking up excitedly with his long tongue flopping out of his mouth. Kieran made a big thing of studying his watch. "Okay, Doggy...ready, steady, go!"

The dog zipped in between four little shrubs, then stuck his nose under the heavy looking plastic sheet and tunnelled his way right under it to the other end. Next, he ran along a log and jumped over the broom that was forming a bridge between two turned up crates. At the bottom of the garden, he ran round the shed, then raced back up to the starting place as fast as his little legs would carry him.

"Nineteen seconds! You've levelled your record, Doggy!" Kieran patted him hard and ruffled the fur on his head like mad, then suddenly tossed his watch over to me and got in the starting position. "Me next. I'm not as good as Doggy, but I've got to try and beat thirty-one seconds. That's my record."

"You mean you're going to do the same course?"

"Uh-huh. It's a good way to get fit, you know. Tell me when to start."

I waited for the second hand to get to the top. "Ready, steady, go!"

Kieran was brilliant at it, even wriggling his way under the sheet. He ran like the wind back up from the shed and wasn't puffing at all.

"Thirty-four!" I yelled out rather babyishly, but I was so excited, I couldn't help it.

"Not bad." He grinned at me. "Your turn."

I got into the starting position full of big determination to beat Kieran. It didn't look all that hard, apart from the tunnel, and I thought I'd try to do that on my elbows like I've seen on army training adverts.

"Get set, go!"

Dodging round the shrubs was more difficult than I'd imagined it would be, and I only just stopped myself from skidding over, then I got down on my stomach and tried to pull myself through the tunnel on my elbows but I wasn't strong enough and it hurt a bit, so I just wriggled as best I could, then tried to get up too soon at the other end, which lost me time.

"Go on, you're doing well," Kieran called.

I stepped up onto the log, but it was more like a craggy old branch that wasn't as flat and level as the beams I was used to walking across in gym. And I lost my balance halfway along and had to step off the side.

"Never mind. Keep going!" yelled Kieran, as though he was my personal trainer. So I ignored the rest of the log and leaped over the broom, then ran as hard as I could round the shed and back up the garden.

"Forty-four," said Kieran. "That's better than *my* first try."

"I didn't realize how hard it is. You make it look really easy."

He grinned at me. "I've had tons of practice."

"Is this how you keep fit?"

"Partly. But I also run round the rec and go

on my blades in the park with Mum and Doggy. Are you thirsty, by the way?"

After we'd had a drink, we spent ages taking turns on the assault course and having goes on the pull-up bar and the speed ball. It was a totally brilliant afternoon.

That night, I lay in bed and stared at the ceiling for ages thinking about Kieran and the assault course and the speed ball and everything. He was so lucky having a proper *barre* in his shed, but I felt really sorry for him having to keep it hidden. It wasn't fair that just because he's a boy he has to keep his ballet a secret. I'm sure if people realized how fit you have to be to do ballet, they wouldn't think it was too girlie for boys to do. My brothers had had another go at me when I'd got home, asking me if Kieran had got little socks to match his little top and saying loads of other horrible things. I started to tell them about his pull-up bar and his speed ball and his assault course, but they were too busy cracking jokes to listen, so I kept quiet in the end. Huh! I'd like to see any of *them* trying to get round that course in less than a minute. They should see Kieran in action. That'd show them.

7 Frozen With Alarm

All through Tuesday at school I kept looking at the clock.

"Can't wait for ballet," I told Poppy excitedly at lunchtime.

"Neither can I," she said, breaking into a huge smile.

I wished I could explain that this was different from the usual way we all three looked forward to ballet. This was an extra burst of *looking-forwardness*. Because of Kieran. But somehow I didn't think Poppy would want to know that.

After school, Mum and I were late setting off for ballet, and that made us get stuck in traffic, so I had to get changed really quickly and didn't have a chance to talk to Kieran at all before class. He was right in front of me on the *barre* and as soon as Miss Coralie told us to turn round to do pliés facing the other way, I waited a second so I could give him a big smile. He must have been concentrating too hard to smile back though and that made my spirits sink a bit.

For the centre work Kieran and I were put in the second row. We went through the usual *port de bras* exercises, then Miss Coralie told Kieran to stand at the side for a moment while the girls tried something on their own. She showed us an exercise with an *arabesque* in it, and I know it seems a bit of a showy-offy thing to say, but I can make my leg go higher than anyone else's in this class so I was really pleased that Kieran would be able to see me do it.

The music started and the feeling of raising my straight leg behind me with my toe pointing up high was the best feeling in the world. I couldn't help glancing over to see if Kieran was watching, but he was doing a stretching exercise and not paying any attention to me at all.

This wasn't what was supposed to happen. I'd been so looking forward to ballet with Kieran, but it was just as though we hardly knew each other again, when I'd thought we were really good friends.

Then Miss Coralie set us a short slow sequence that included a *développé* to the side and I thought of a way of getting Kieran's attention without being noticed. A way that would get him back for tickling my leg with his ballet shoe at Poppy's house on Saturday. With a *développé* you have to lift your knee first, then unfold your leg to a pointed toe, while you're balancing on a turned-out foot. We were facing the corner for that part of the exercise and I deliberately moved forwards a little bit, so that when I extended my leg, my toe touched Kieran's shoulder, but I pretended I didn't realize. I thought Kieran would find it quite funny, but also be impressed with how high I'd made my leg go.

Well, I don't know if it was for a joke or not, but he nudged my foot off quite hard with his shoulder and I lost my balance and went crashing into the girl next to me, which made her lose *her* balance and knock into the girl on the end of the row. We must have looked like dominoes tumbling down.

Miss Coralie's eyes flashed in a worried way, at first. But then, when she was sure no one was hurt, she spoke in a low warning voice. "I don't know what exactly happened just then, Kieran and Rose, but I trust it was an accident. Be very careful in future, you two." She paused, but kept her eyes on us. "All right?"

I nodded and when Miss Coralie went over

to open the skylight window with the long pole, I tried giving Kieran a grin. I didn't get one back, though, because he wasn't even looking at me. I thought he must want to be left alone, but if I left him alone during school time *and* during ballet, I'd only ever get to be his friend at the weekend. And that seemed really silly. So I waited till it came to jumps, made sure Miss Coralie wasn't watching, then nudged him and whispered, "I've been practising, so watch out!"

"When you've finished talking, Rose..."

I must have spoken a bit more loudly than a whisper after all, because Miss Coralie's hands were on her waist and her head was tilted to one side with her eyebrows arched as though she'd been waiting for ages for me to stop talking. I quickly stood up straight to show I was ready, but then Emily turned round and looked at me like I was pathetic. And I couldn't get the look out of my head, so it stopped me from concentrating properly when Miss Coralie gave us the sequence. I was frantically marking it through with my hands, trying to remember what came after the *soubresauts* when she suddenly said, "And..."

All the way through the sequence, I was a step behind everyone else.

"That's what happens when you talk, Rose." Miss Coralie fixed me with one of her strictest looks. "Let's go through it again."

This time I got it perfectly, thank goodness, and I thought I was jumping as high as Kieran, but only because the music was quite quick and if either of us had jumped any higher we would have been behind the beat. I snapped my knees tight and stood up straight at the end of the exercise, and Miss Coralie turned to Mrs. Marsden.

"Could we have it a fraction slower this time, please?" That meant that Miss Coralie thought we could manage to spring higher. She was concentrating on showing Mrs. Marsden the speed she wanted with her hand so I quickly nudged Kieran and he gave me half a smile.

I suppose I was just so happy Kieran had actually smiled at me that before I knew it I'd blurted out, "Game on!" and stuck out my hand to shake on it.

"Rose!" Miss Coralie's voice gave me a shock.

In a flash I pulled my hand back. "Sorry."

"I'm getting more than a bit fed up with this, you know."

It was obvious she was furious.

I croaked out another little "sorry" then stood as stiff as a poker, which was supposed to be my way of showing that I was back to my best concentration.

"And now look at you. That's how you used to stand when you first joined this class." Her voice turned cold. The room was completely silent. "I've noticed your attitude changing recently, Rose. You were supposed to be taking grade four this term, but clearly I've made a mistake putting you in for it. You'd obviously much rather mess around than learn ballet."

Her eyes bored into me and I tried to unstiffen my body, but how could I, when I was frozen with alarm? It was a horrible, horrible moment and I knew my face was going pale. Her words were whizzing round my head... *Made a mistake putting you in for it... Made a mistake putting you in for it...*

I didn't look at Kieran once till the end of the lesson. And Miss Coralie didn't look at me. No wonder. She wasn't interested in me any more, now that I wasn't one of the exam candidates. I kept on searching for her eyes so she could see how hard I was trying, but she was always looking at Emily or Becky or one of the others.

When we'd done the *révérence* and Kieran had done a bow, Miss Coralie said she wanted a word with Kieran and I hoped she wasn't going to tell him off, because he shouldn't be blamed for anything. It was all my fault.

Out in the corridor I went back into my frozen state. What had I done? It was terrible. Absolutely terrible. Then I heard someone whispering my name, and realized that Jazz and Poppy were looking at me with big eyes.

"Are you okay?" asked Poppy in an urgent sort of hiss.

I nodded and tried to smile, but I couldn't. They'd been completely right about me getting distracted. And now I'd gone and ruined everything. Miss Coralie had taken me out of the exam. Why, oh why, hadn't I realized that Kieran had had enough of me? Especially when he'd clearly told me he wasn't going to muck about any more because he was here to learn ballet. What an idiot I'd been, carrying on and on, and trying to attract his attention.

Feeling the most miserable I'd felt for ages, I wandered into the changing room with the rest of the girls, and got changed really slowly because my body seemed too heavy to move any faster. I was almost the last one to go, and the staircase was totally empty, but I didn't have the energy to be a bird this week, so I just walked down with ploddy feet, listening to the scrunchy little echo that your footsteps make on the stone steps.

When I pulled open the heavy door at the bottom, the sunlight gave me a shock, as if a sort of darkness had crept inside me with Miss Coralie's terrible words, making the bright daylight too startling to bear.

8 Emergency Meeting

The next week was one of the worst of my life. It was impossible to bear the thought that I wouldn't be taking grade four this term and I was desperate to talk to Poppy and Jasmine to ask them if they thought there was anything at all that might make Miss Coralie change her mind, but I didn't dare tell them what had happened. They'd be so disappointed and cross with me, and say "We *told* you", and then they'd start leaving me out of the triplegang, because they'd be fed up of waiting for me to pass grade four and move up into their class.

If only I could turn back the clock and do the last ballet lesson all over again. In fact, it would be safer if I could do the last *three* lessons again and be on my best behaviour and never look at Kieran one single time. But I'd spoiled everything now and there was no going back. And what would happen when Mum and Dad found out? They'd be furious with me for wasting their money and mucking about when I should have been concentrating. Whenever I had these thoughts, which was nearly all the time, I closed my eyes with horror and felt myself sinking down into a hole of despair.

Then I realized that if I didn't tell Poppy and Jasmine what had happened, they'd find out on their own in the end and that would make them like me even less for keeping such a big thing from them. And it was true, there'd been loads of break times and lunchtimes at school when I could have told Poppy, but somehow I never quite had enough courage.

On Saturday morning, though, I woke up absolutely determined to talk to them both that afternoon at Jazz's house. I worked out the exact words I would say and I practised them all through the morning. When the afternoon came I got them ready loads of times, but every time I opened my mouth they refused to come out.

"What, Rose?" asked Jasmine. "I keep thinking you're going to say something."

But I just turned up my palms and gave her a puzzled look as though I didn't know why on earth she thought that.

And so the afternoon came and went without me telling them.

When I got home I found myself wanting to cry. I *never* cry though, so I just went back down into my hole of despair.

On Monday at school I tried again, but the teacher kept us in late when the bell went for morning break, and when I got out Poppy was with some other girls from her class, so I just joined in their conversation. Then at lunchtime Poppy had choir and I had gym club, and there was no time left afterwards.

After school I lay on my bed and stared at the ceiling with my thumbs pressed against each other, whispering *Please make something lucky happen,* over and over again. But all that happened was that the phone rang. It turned out to be Poppy asking me if I could bring into school my special Russian doll that granny had bought for my birthday, because her class were doing something about dolls in art.

"Yes, course I can. And I've got something to tell you..."

There. I'd said it. I'd actually said it. And I hadn't even been meaning to.

"What? You sound a bit worried. Are you all right?"

There was no going back now. "I can't tell you on the phone. It's...serious."

"Rose, you're scaring me now! Just tell me

what it's about."

"Miss..."

"Miss Coralie?"

I nodded, but of course Poppy couldn't hear that.

"*Is* it Miss Coralie?"

"Yes." It came out like a little squeak.

"Was she cross in the last lesson? Is that why you looked so worried when you came out?"

"Yes." Another squeak.

"What, *really* cross?"

"Yes. She said I couldn't do..."

Poppy's voice went into a squeal of alarm. "She didn't...say you couldn't do grade four, did she?"

I hardly dared to answer, but Poppy had practically got it out of me anyway.

My voice was no more than a whisper. "Yes."

There was a huge gasp on the other end of the phone and then silence. I shut my eyes again and felt myself falling back down into that hole of despair.

"Look, I'll phone Jasmine, okay? And…and let's see what she says."

I could hardly manage to speak now. "Okay."

When I'd disconnected I took the phone up to my room and lay on the bed clutching it.

About two minutes later it rang and I quickly answered it before Mum could. It was Jazz speaking at about a hundred miles an hour.

"Poppy says you can't do grade four. Did Miss Coralie actually say that? What *exactly* did she say?"

"She said… She said…"

"What?"

"She said she'd made a mistake putting me in for it because of my attitude. Then she didn't look at me again for the rest of the lesson."

There was a pause. And the pause got longer and longer. I began to wonder if Jasmine had chucked the phone down on her bed in disgust and walked away, leaving me hanging on the other end.

"Jazz?"

"Don't worry, Rose. We'll sort it out."

And because her voice was gentle and kind, I felt like bursting into tears again, and my throat hurt when I tried to swallow.

"Look, my dad's away," she went on. "I'll ask my mum if I can come round to your house just for a few minutes. I'll pretend I've got to borrow...your Russian doll. Yes, that's a good idea. I'll say we're doing a project on traditional dolls for school... And I'll phone Poppy back and say it's fine."

"What's fine?"

"Fine to come over to your place. That's what she phoned me for. She said you were in a state and you needed us."

When I'd said bye to Jasmine I *did* cry, because I was so lucky to have such good friends. Poppy and Jazz had straight away thought of coming to see me as soon as they knew I was in trouble.

✳

Twenty minutes later, Poppy's mum turned up with Poppy, and Jazz's mum arrived with Jazz, and all the mums laughed and agreed that it was an amazing coincidence that Poppy and Jazz both wanted to borrow exactly the same thing off me for school at exactly the same time. And everyone said it was very nice of Jazz to let Poppy take it, and manage with just drawing a picture of it, which was the plan we'd made seeing as Jazz didn't actually need it.

"Come and have a cup of tea while you're waiting for Jasmine to do her picture," Mum said to the two other mums.

The three of us rushed up to my room, closed the door and just sat on the floor in a little circle. Jasmine and Poppy were looking at me, waiting to hear what I had to say.

I took a deep breath and told them the whole story. I finished by saying that I knew I'd been stupid and I'd just had the worst week of my life and I was dreading going to ballet the next day because I hated it when Miss Coralie didn't even look at me. And then I sighed and shut up.

Both of them looked so sorry for me that I wished I'd told them ages before.

"I think you should write her a letter," Jazz suddenly said.

A big wave of fear swept over me. "What would I put?"

"Put what you feel," said Poppy.

"I can't. It won't be grown up enough."

"It doesn't have to be grown up. It just has to be what you feel."

"Yes," said Jasmine, jumping up. "Now where's your paper?"

"I've only got notelets."

She grabbed the packet, took one out and gave me a pen from my desk. "Go on."

"Say what you feel," Poppy reminded me.

I sighed and started writing. It didn't take me long. Then I read it out loud.

Dear Miss Coralie,

I'm very very very very sorry for messing about in ballet. I feel stupid and gilty, but most of all very very very very sad about not being aloud to take grade 4. I will never even look at Kieran any more and I hope you will forgive me for my bad attitude.

Yours sincerely,
Rose.

As soon as I'd finished reading, I wanted to tear it up and try again because it didn't sound like a proper letter. But Jazz and Poppy both said it was very good indeed. Jazz read it through herself and said I'd made two spelling mistakes, but she didn't think they'd matter.

"Now, this is what you've got to do with it," she went on. "When you run in at the beginning of class, just pop it on the piano, then go straight to the *barre* and get into position and don't even look at her. She'll think it's a note from your mum and she won't read it till the end of the lesson..."

"And then what?" My voice had come out in a bit of a babyish wail because I didn't like it when Jazz ran out of ideas.

"And then...next week, she'll probably forgive you," said Poppy quickly.

"Probably?"

"Yes," said Jazz. "And start looking at you again...and...it'll all be back to normal."

But neither of them had said anything about the most important thing of all.

I hardly dared ask. "Do you think Miss Coralie might change her mind and let me do grade four then?"

Poppy and Jazz exchanged a look. It was Jazz who spoke. "She might be...kind of...trying to teach you a lesson, you see."

Poppy looked at the floor and Jazz started biting her lip.

"You mean, she'll have to stick to what she said or I won't learn my lesson?"

Jazz nodded.

I snatched back my letter and quickly added, *P.S. I have definutly learned my lesson.*

The other two read what I'd written but didn't say anything so I had to ask if they thought it was okay.

Poppy just nodded, and Jazz said, "That makes three spelling mistakes, but never mind."

And a moment later Mum called upstairs that Jazz's and Poppy's mums were ready to go.

"Thumb-thumb! Quick!" said Poppy.

We stood in a little circle, touching thumbs. I stayed silent and so did Jazz, but Poppy whispered, "Please let Miss Coralie be kind."

Then I hugged them both for being such good friends and Jazz did the fastest drawing ever of my Russian doll.

9 The Lesson

The next day I got more and more nervous as the hours passed and by the time it was ballet my hands were shaking so much I couldn't even do my hair properly. Every time I scraped it back to put it in a ponytail there was another bump in it. In the line in the corridor, my legs were all trembly. I was holding my card in its envelope tight by my side, and so far no one had spotted it. Kieran came out of his changing room and joined the back of the line but I didn't even turn round.

"Come in, class," called Miss Coralie. And

we all ran in on tiptoe.

I did exactly what Jazz had told me to do and went straight to the piano. I knew Miss Coralie and Mrs. Marsden were both watching me because I could feel their eyes on me, but I didn't look at either of them, just put the card on the top of the piano and ran on tiptoe to a place on the *barre,* pulled up out of my ribs as we've been taught and stared straight ahead.

We started with *pliés* and I turned out as hard as I could, and concentrated on keeping my arms soft and pressing my heels into the ground. I was so hoping that Miss Coralie might say, "Nice, Rose," because I felt sure these were the best *pliés* I'd ever done, but she didn't say anything and that made me a bit anxious.

For the rest of the *barre* I kept reminding myself what Jazz and Poppy had said. It didn't matter that Miss Coralie wasn't saying a single word to me. It was all part of the lesson she was trying to teach me, and by next week everything would be back to normal.

When we had to do *arabesques* I made my leg go as high as possible without turning my hip, and that was when Miss Coralie finally spoke to me.

"Good, Rose."

I felt like smiling round at everyone when she said that, I was so happy, but I knew how important it was to stay totally focused, so I carried on staring straight ahead as I closed in my foot at the back.

I got a "nice" during the jumps and Kieran got three. I wondered if he was counting, but I still didn't look in his direction one single time, not even at the end of the lesson when he did his bow and we did our *révérence*. Miss Coralie told us all we could go and as I turned to join the line I saw her pick up my card.

"One second, Rose, please."

I stopped in my tracks, but wasn't sure what

I was supposed to do because she was holding my card ready to read it, but had just called out to the grade fives to come in. Jazz and Poppy both gave me the teeniest smiles from the *barre*, then stood perfectly straight and stared straight ahead of them. I was standing right in the middle of the room looking at the floor while Miss Coralie read my card, and I expect the rest of the girls were probably wondering why on earth I hadn't gone out with the other grade fours.

A moment later Miss Coralie called me over, but instead of speaking to me, she turned to Mrs. Marsden and nodded, then looked at the grade fives and said, "*Pliés*. And..."

Mrs. Marsden began to play the music much more loudly than usual so I had to go quite close to Miss Coralie to hear what she was saying.

"I agree with you, Rose."

I wasn't sure what she meant and my mind

was full of confused thoughts, so I just said, "Pardon?"

"I agree that you've definitely learned your lesson. You didn't have to write that down because you showed me all through class."

"Sorry," I said.

"No, I'm *glad* you wrote it, all the same."

Then she actually smiled at me and did a little signal to Mrs. Marsden to keep playing. And as the grade fives kept silently working, the music drowned out Miss Coralie's words for everyone except me, and I felt as though I was in a dream. "I shall keep your card in my memory box, and when you're a famous ballerina I'll take it out and look at it, and think, *Hmmm, I remember when that girl first joined my class and she didn't realize how she was supposed to behave, and she didn't actually want to be in the class anyway because she preferred doing gym, and then suddenly she had a complete change of heart and started to* dedicate herself to ballet and all was going fine until one day a boy joined the class and she went back to her old ways, but thank goodness it turned out to be only a blip, and here's the card that marks the end of that blip."

It was funny because Miss Coralie was saying the best words in the world and yet I was getting another one of those lumps in my throat as though I wanted to cry. Maybe it was because she hadn't mentioned the exam. Yes, that was it. She still hadn't told me if I was allowed to do the exam. That must mean that nothing had changed, so Jazz and Poppy were right about that. I'd just have to be patient and wait another term. It was my own fault. I deserved it.

And then the *plié* music finished and Miss Coralie looked up. She'd obviously finished talking to me.

"Thank you very much," I whispered as I turned to go. Then I shot out as fast as I could so I wouldn't be disturbing the class any more.

But when I was at the door she called out again and her voice sounded strict and sharp in the silence.

"Rose!"

I just knew that every single person in the room would be looking at me as I turned round slowly. My heartbeat sped up when I saw her disapproving expression.

But then her eyes twinkled. "I do hope you're not going to run like that when you do your exam in a couple of weeks' time!"

Something zinged inside my body and I wanted to jump for joy, then race round the room yelling out, "I'm taking grade four! I'm taking grade four!" But all I did was break into a big smile for Miss Coralie, then swish it over to Poppy and Jazz. They both looked as though they were going to burst with excitement and I knew I'd be looking exactly the same.

"*Battements glissés*," said Miss Coralie, bringing us back to earth.

Every single head faced front.

"And…"

The music started – quieter this time – and I crept out.

10 Friends For Ever

For days and days after the exam all I wanted to do was talk about it to Poppy and Jazz, going over every single minute and wondering how I'd got on, but it was impossible to tell. I was really looking forward to seeing Kieran, who was coming round to my house on Sunday afternoon, as we never even looked at each other in ballet classes any more. We often talked in school though, and it didn't matter that the boys had found out that Kieran did ballet. No one ever teased him *or* me about it. They must have realized at long last that there's nothing wrong with ballet. I knew that some of the boys had been to Kieran's house, so I guessed they'd tried out his assault course and his pull-up bar and seen how fit and strong he is compared to them.

At lunchtime on Sunday I started to get excited because Poppy and Jazz were coming over too and I just knew we were going to have a good time. The only thing spoiling my excitement was the thought that my brothers might be around. So as soon as lunch finished, I asked them the big question as casually as possible.

"Are you going out this afternoon?"

"Dunno," said Rory. "I might just watch the match on telly." He got up to clear his plate away. "Are you going to watch it, Jack?"

"Dunno."

Very helpful.

"I was going to get Josh round," said Adam.

My eyes widened. *No! No! I want less people, not more!*

"But I might go to his house instead."

Phew!

"I'll watch the match with you," said Jack. "There's nothing else to do."

Mum gave me a little smile and shrugged her shoulders as the doorbell rang. She knew I was hoping my brothers wouldn't be around while Kieran was over here. As it happened it was Poppy and Jazz at the door, and the first thing we did was go up to my room and talk about the exam all over again. The trouble was, the only part I could clearly remember was running in and standing in line with Emily and Becky, doing our curtseys for the examiner, and saying, "Good morning Miss Frazer," and thinking how smart and official she looked, and hearing her check our names, then ask us to go to the *barre*. After that it was all a bit of a blur because I'd been concentrating so hard the whole time that there hadn't been even a millimetre of brain left to notice whether I was doing it well or not! So, as usual, our conversation finished up with Jazz and Poppy asking me the same questions, me not knowing the answers and then getting nervous and saying, "What if I don't even get a C?" and them saying, "Don't be silly. Course you will." That was all I wanted. Just a C, because it's so difficult to get an A or a B. But the more time went by, the more I got myself into a state, worrying in case I didn't pass at all.

We were looking out of my bedroom window, waiting for Kieran to arrive, when Poppy suddenly said, "Just think, you might hear your result on Tuesday!"

My legs turned straight to jelly as they always did when I thought about getting my result. Miss Coralie had said it would take about three weeks, so it could be any time now.

"Kieran's late," said Jazz, changing the subject. "Shall we go and do some ballet?"

But I desperately wanted to get my mind off the exam and I'd suddenly had a good idea exactly how to do that. "Let's make an assault course."

Poppy went a bit pink. "As long as *I* don't have to do it. I'd be hopeless."

"Me too," said Jazz, "but I don't mind trying." So we all went downstairs and out into the back garden.

"We could use the branch that hangs down. It's quite thick and strong," I said.

"And we could get a skipping rope and make that part of the course," said Poppy. "I wouldn't mind doing that bit."

So together we carried on thinking of things and in the end we worked out that first you had to do ten skips of the skipping rope, then ten step-ups on an upside-down crate, then you had to run round the clothes line and back to the hanging-down branch. After you'd done four pull-ups on that, you came to the thick plastic sheet, and when you'd gone underneath it, you ran over to the three chairs, which were side by side, scrambled over the seats, then leaped or stepped over the seat of the swing, before the last sprint back to the start.

"Now we just need a stopwatch."

"What are you lot doing?" Adam called out from the back door.

"I thought you were going to Josh's," I called back.

"He's ill. What are you doing?"

"An assault course," said Jazz, who was really getting into it. "We're going to time ourselves."

"*I'm* not," said Poppy quietly.

I put my arm round her. "No one's making you."

And next thing Adam was out in the garden with us, handing me his watch. "Right, tell me what to do."

We explained it all to him and I told him when to start, then off he zoomed. He thought he was doing so brilliantly but compared to the way I'd seen Kieran doing Doggy's assault course, Adam was rubbish. He had to abandon the skipping because he kept tripping over the rope, and he only managed two pull-ups, which made him mad. By the time he was running to the swing at the end you could tell he was really tired, even though he tried to hide it.

"One minute and thirty-two seconds," I told him.

"That skipping lost me loads of time," he puffed. "You ought to get rid of that bit. It's too girlie."

"Boxers skip when they're training," Jazz informed him.

Adam just grunted and started complaining about the pull-ups instead. "I'd like to see *you* lot doing them!"

Jasmine went next and it took her a bit longer, which made Adam relieved, I could tell. She found the skipping easy, but only managed one pull-up, then lost quite a lot of time getting under the sheet. Poppy said she'd have a go later, and I knew it was because she didn't want to do it in front of Adam, so I told him to leave us alone, but he insisted on staying to watch me have a go. What's more, Jack and Rory both came out as well because it was half-time in the match.

"Go on, Rose," called Jack. "Let's see you do it."

I didn't feel like it now. "*You* do it."

Jack was quite good, apart from kicking one of the chairs over by mistake. He could only do three pull-ups, trembling and straining like mad, but pretending it was easy. "I could cut that time down by loads if I practised it," he said, flopping over, exhausted.

Then we all clearly heard the ring at the front door.

"I'll get it."

As I raced inside, I heard Jasmine telling the boys who it was, and I also heard Rory do a massive laugh. "Maybe Twinkle Toes can show us how it's done!"

And after my heart had sunk down to my socks, it came pinging back up again. *Yes*, I thought, with a surge of excitement. *Yes, maybe he can!*

"You look happy!" said Kieran, as I opened the door.

"I am!" I replied. "We've set up this brilliant assault course." I rushed ahead of him through the kitchen to the back garden, where I pointed quickly to each of my brothers. "Jack, Rory, Adam." Then I thought I'd better finish the introduction off properly. "And this is Kieran."

"Hi, Kieran," they all said exactly together.

"And this is the assault course," I added for Kieran's benefit.

"Pleased to meet you, assault course," said Kieran, which made everyone laugh, even Rory, who thinks he's the only person in the world who can crack a joke.

He and Adam were staring at Kieran. I don't think they'd been expecting a boy with a

number-one haircut, jeans with holes in them and
a T-shirt that said *STRIKING EAGLES* on it.

"Have a go, Kieran," said Jack.

"It's okay. Someone else can go first," Kieran
said straight away.

Poppy was definitely far too shy to go, so I
said I would. As soon as Rory said the word "go"
I ran to the skipping rope and did ten skips in a
flash. My whole body felt light and strong as
though I'd be able to fly if that had been part of
the course. The step-ups seemed easier than
usual and I zipped round the clothes line and
sprang up to grasp hold of the branch. But I
could only do two pull-ups because my arms
were too trembly.

"Weakling!" called Adam, and that filled
me with another burst of determination. The
skin on my arms and my stomach burned as I
scraped my way under the heavy plastic sheet.

"Not bad, Rose," Jack said, winking at me.

"That's because ballet makes you fit," Jazz

told him as I ran over the chairs, then the swing seat and back to the start position.

"One minute three seconds," said Rory in a grumpy voice. "It's all right for girls. They're always skipping. And Rose is so titchy it gives her an unfair advantage."

"You have a go, Kieran," was all I said.

Then it went quiet as Kieran took his place at the start. I stood right back out of the way, and Poppy and Jasmine came over to stand by me. Adam nudged Rory and they exchanged a big grin.

"Hope he shows them!" whispered Poppy in quite a fierce voice for her.

"So do I," said Jazz, sticking up her thumb. And quick as a flash we all did a thumb-thumb for good luck for Kieran.

Then, "Go!" said Rory. And Kieran was off.

When he skipped his feet hardly left the ground and the rope turned so fast it was a blur. The way he did the step-ups, you'd think the crate was about two centimetres high. After he'd run round the clothes line, he sprang up to the branch and did one, two, three, four, five pull-ups, easy as patting your knees, then called down to us, "How many of these did you say you had to do?"

"Four!" I called back and he dropped down immediately and shot under the sheet and out the other end almost as fast as Doggy could have done. I saw Rory's mouth hanging open and Adam's eyes bulging and Jack shaking his head as he whispered, "Incredible!" Then Kieran ran over the chairs, leaped over the swing and darted back to the start.

He wasn't even puffing when he asked what his time had been.

"Forty-three," said Rory. Then he frowned at the watch for ages before he repeated, "Yeah...forty-three seconds."

I couldn't help feeling pleased with what I said next, even though it was rather sarcastic.

"What was it you were saying about male ballet dancers not being as fit as footballers, Rory?"

Kieran threw back his head and laughed. "Everyone says that!"

Rory shuffled about a bit, then said, "Yeah, but you train, don't you, Kieran? Otherwise, how do you manage all the skipping and those pull-ups and things?"

"That's all part of my ballet training," said Kieran. "You need to have strength, stamina and suppleness to get anywhere in ballet."

All my brothers looked embarrassed then because they didn't know what to say to a boy who talked about ballet. I felt as though I was getting a little peek inside their minds and watching all their stupid thoughts about male dancers crumbling away. It was brilliant.

"Show us how you skip like that," Adam said. And the next minute, Kieran was giving Adam a skipping lesson, while Jack was practising step-ups and Rory was straining away trying to do more than two pull-ups.

We watched them for a bit, and noticed that Adam soon got puffed out from skipping. He'd obviously completely changed his mind about Kieran though, because he started asking him lots of questions about ballet.

"Not watching the second half of the match, boys?" Mum said to Jack and Rory. Then she handed me the phone. "It's for you, Rose."

I hadn't even heard it ringing. I took it from Mum, thinking it was probably Granny, but then I got a shock.

"Hello, Rose. It's Miss Coralie."

"Hello," I said, feeling my legs turning to jelly again.

"I've been away this weekend, but I've just got back to find the results waiting for me. Congratulations, Rose. You got the top mark – A. I always knew you could do it. I'm so proud of you!"

Now I understand what people mean about waiting for the words to sink in, because that's what happened with me just then in our back garden. I could hear all the others saying, "What? Who is it? What's happened, Rose?" and I realized I must have looked like a ghost in shock from seeing another ghost.

"Th-th-thank you," I managed to stutter out. Then the words truly sank in. "Thank you so so so much. I'm so excited."

"Go off and celebrate, Rose. You deserve it! And I'll see you on Tuesday."

"Yes. Thank you. And thank you again."

I knew I sounded like a little kid, but I couldn't help it. I gave the phone back to Mum and started leaping round the garden, swinging on the branch and the actual swing. Poppy and Jazz must have guessed it was Miss Coralie, and came running over to me.

"Just tell us what you got!" said Jazz, grabbing my arm to stop me flying around.

"A!" I cried out at the top of my voice, so people six gardens down the road would have been able to hear me.

"A!" shrieked Jazz and Poppy at the same time. "That's absolutely brilliant!"

And then we were all three flying round the garden. Mum rushed over to give me a big hug and even the boys said, "Hey, well done, Ro!"

Kieran stuck his thumbs up. "That's brilliant, Rose!"

"Shall we go and watch the rest of the match?" said Rory, and in they all went, including Kieran.

A bit later, when we three had calmed down a bit, and Kieran was still indoors with my brothers, Poppy and Jazz and I sat down together in the middle of the lawn.

"We're all going to be together again in class now," said Poppy happily. "It's going to be so fantastic."

"Truly triplegang!" I said, which made the others laugh.

But then Jazz turned serious. "It's funny to think that there's a whole big future for all of us, just waiting for us to live it, isn't it?" she said thoughtfully.

"I wonder if we'll always be friends," said Poppy.

"And if our ballerina dreams *will* come true," added Jazz.

"Yes, definitely," I told them, feeling very sure of myself now.

"Yes, definitely friends for ever, you mean?" asked Poppy.

"Friends for ever *and* dancing for ever," I told her.

Then we closed our eyes, pressed our thumbs together and spoke at exactly the same time. "Friends for ever. And dancing for ever."

Basic Ballet Positions

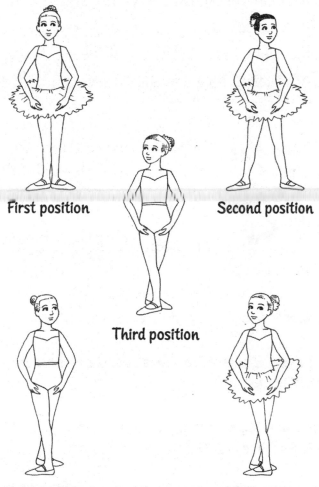

First position

Second position

Third position

Fourth position

Fifth position

Ballet words are mostly in French, which makes them more magical. But when you're learning, it's nice to know what they mean too. Here are some of the words that all Miss Coralie's students have to learn:

adage The name for the slow steps in the centre of the room, away from the *barre*.

arabesque A beautiful balance on one leg.

assemblé A jump where the feet come together at the end.

battement dégagé A foot exercise at the *barre* to get beautiful toes.

battement tendu Another foot exercise where you stretch your foot until it points.

chassé A soft smooth slide of the feet.

développé A lifting and unfolding of one leg into the air, while balancing on the other.

fifth position croisé When you are facing, say the *left* corner, with your feet in fifth position, and your front foot is the *right* foot.

fouetté This step is so fast your feet are in a blur! You do it to prepare for *pirouettes*.

grand battement High kick!

jeté A spring where you land on the opposite foot. Rose loves these!

pas de bourrée Tiny little steps to the side, like a mouse.

pas de chat A cat hop from one foot to the other.

plié This is the first step we do in class. You have to bend your knees slowly and make sure your feet are turned right out, with your heels firmly planted on the floor for as long as possible.

port de bras Arm movements, which Poppy is good at.

révérence The curtsey at the end of class.

rond de jambe This is where you make a circle with your leg.

sissonne A scissor step.

sissonne en arrière A scissor step going backwards. This is really hard!

sissonne en avant A scissor step going forwards.

soubresaut A jump off two feet, pointing your feet hard in the air.

temps levé A step and sweep up the other leg then jump.

turnout You have to stand with your legs and feet and hips all opened out and pointing to the side, not the front. This is the most important thing in ballet that everyone learns right from the start.

If you love ballet, you might be interested
in these other ballet books:

ISBN PB 0 7460 5593 5
HB 0 7460 5594 3

ISBN 0 7460 1692 1

ISBN 0 7460 5899 3

Ballerina Dreams

Poppy's Secret Wish
0 7460 6024 6

Jasmine's Lucky Star
0 7460 6025 4

Rose's Big Decision
0 7460 6026 2

Dancing Princess
0 7460 6433 0

Dancing with the Stars
0 7460 6434 9

Dancing For Ever
0 7460 6435 7

All books are priced at £3.99